D1062304

PLEASE WASH
YOUR HANDS
BEFORE YOU READ ME
AND KEEP ME CLEAN

THE
CLOWN'S
SMILE

THE CLOWN'S SMILE
by Mike Thaler
illustrations by Tracey Cameron
Harper & Row, Publishers

The Clown's Smile

10 9 8 7 6 5 4 3 2 1
First Edition

Library of Congress Cataloging-in-Publication Data
Thaler, Mike, date
The clown's smile.

Summary: An elusive smile flies from clown to acrobat to lion tamer to other people at the circus, until the clown's crying prompts its return.
[1. Clowns—Fiction. 2. Circus—Fiction. 3. Smile—Fiction] I. Cameron, Tracey, ill. II. Title.
PZ7.T3C1 1986 [E] 85-45850
ISBN 0-06-026051-3
ISBN 0-06-026052-1 (lib. bdg.)

In loving memory of
Boris and Riva Deutsch

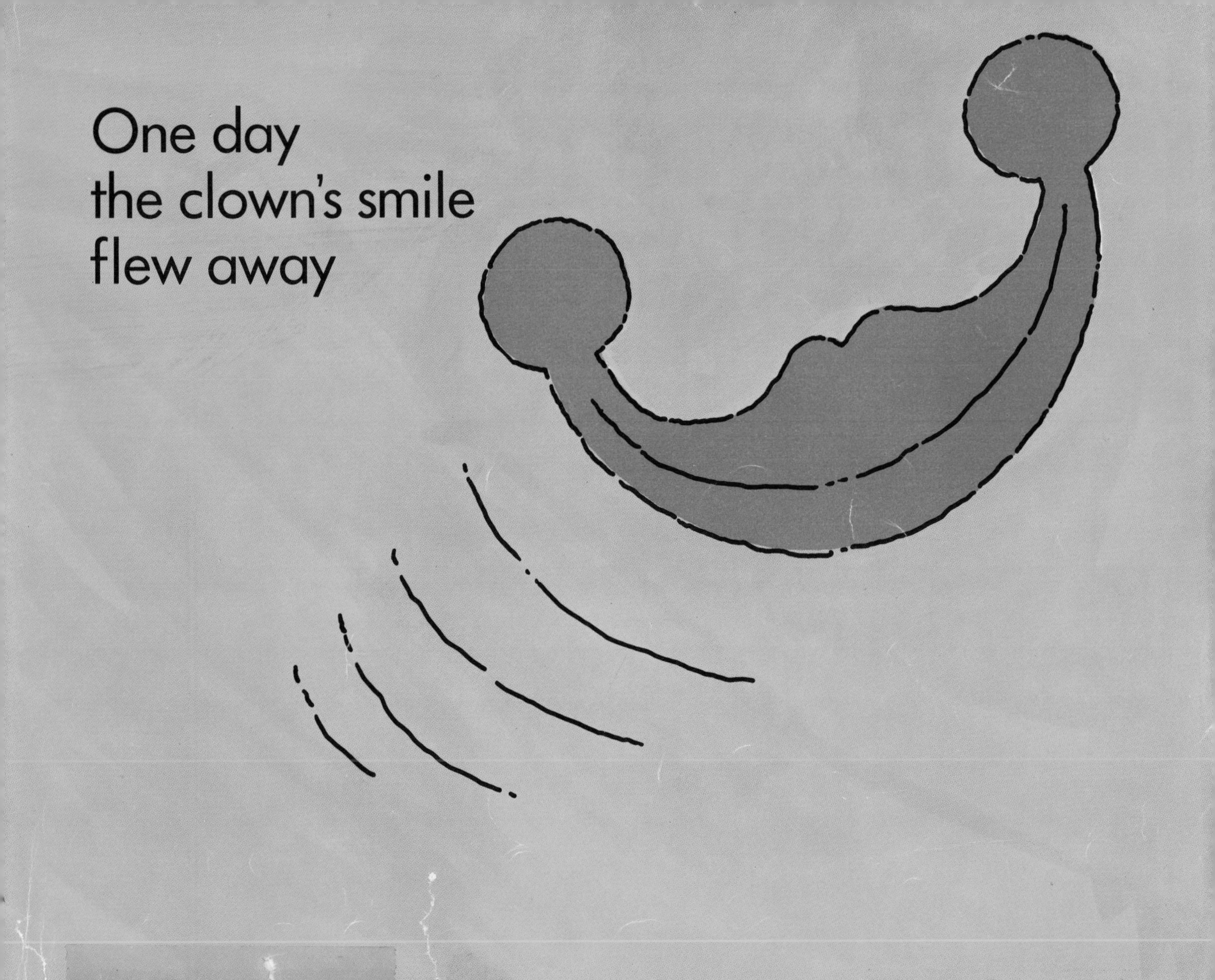
One day
the clown's smile
flew away

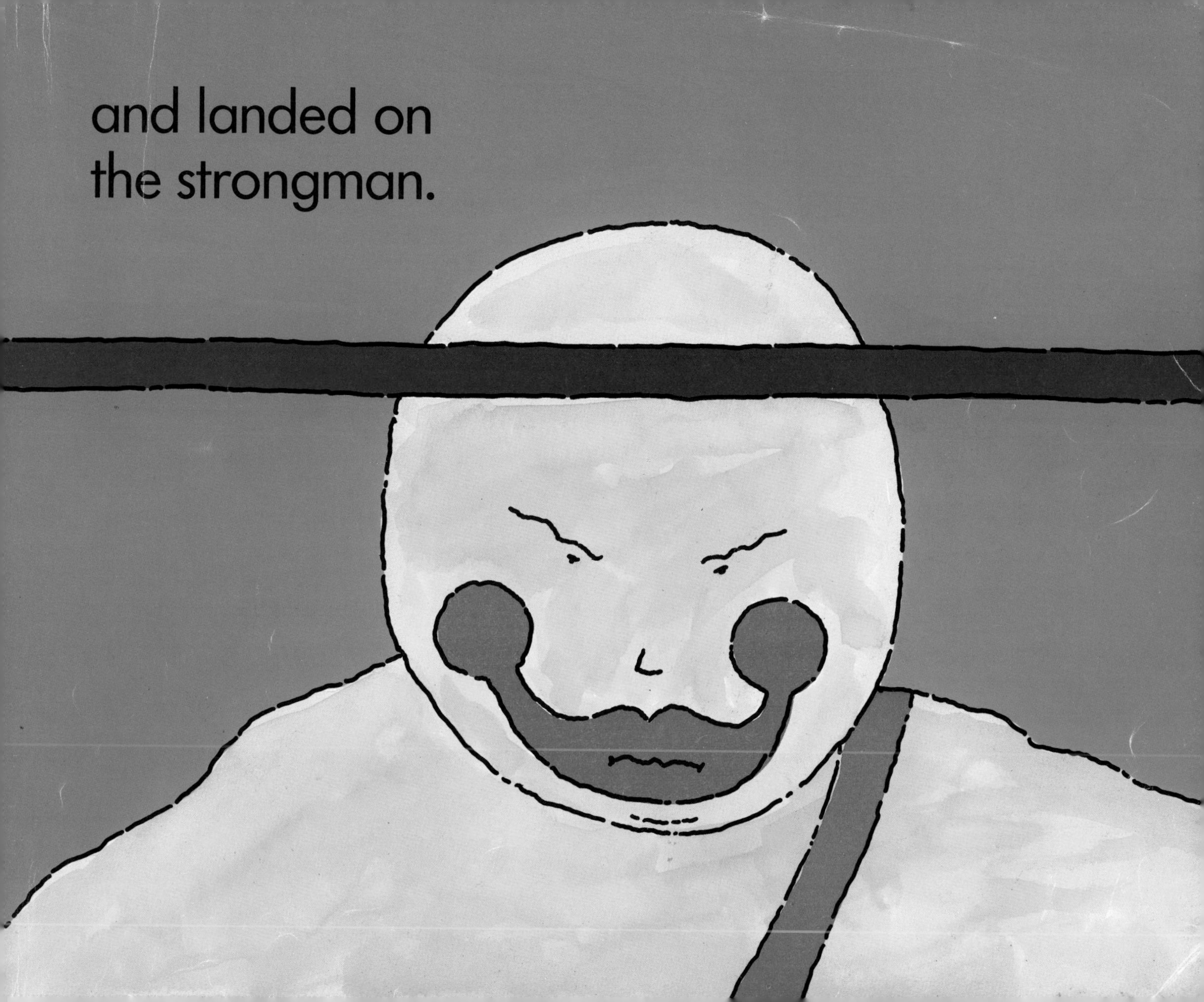

and landed on
the strongman.

Then it flew to
the fat lady
and the thin man,

the bareback rider,

then the horse.

The clown
ran after it,

but it was too fast
for him,
and it flew up
to the acrobat,

then
down
to
the
lion
tamer
and
the
lion

and the elephant.

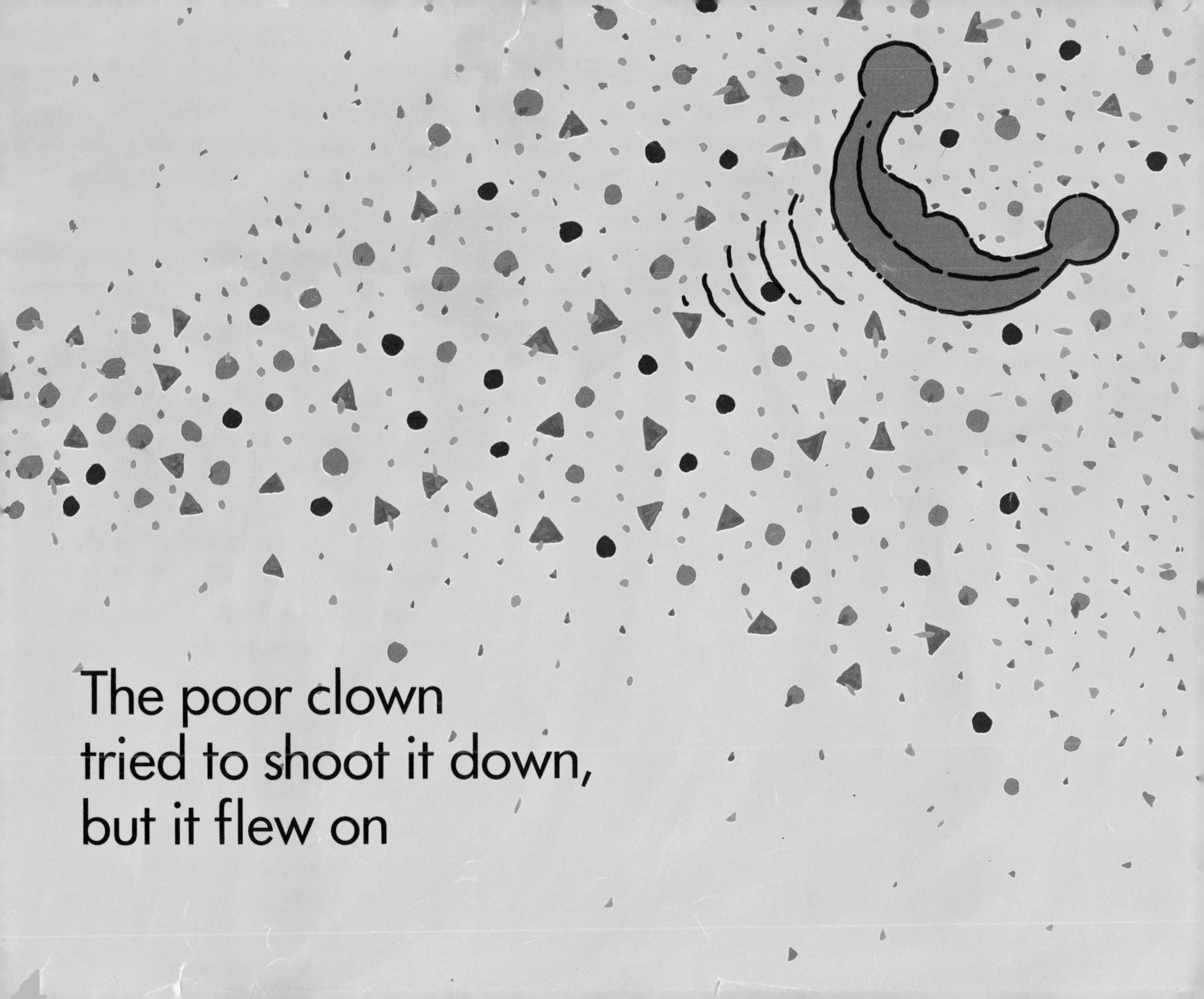

The poor clown
tried to shoot it down,
but it flew on

to the gorilla,

to the mayor in the audience,
to the mayor's wife,

to the bearded lady,

to the snake,

to the snake charmer,

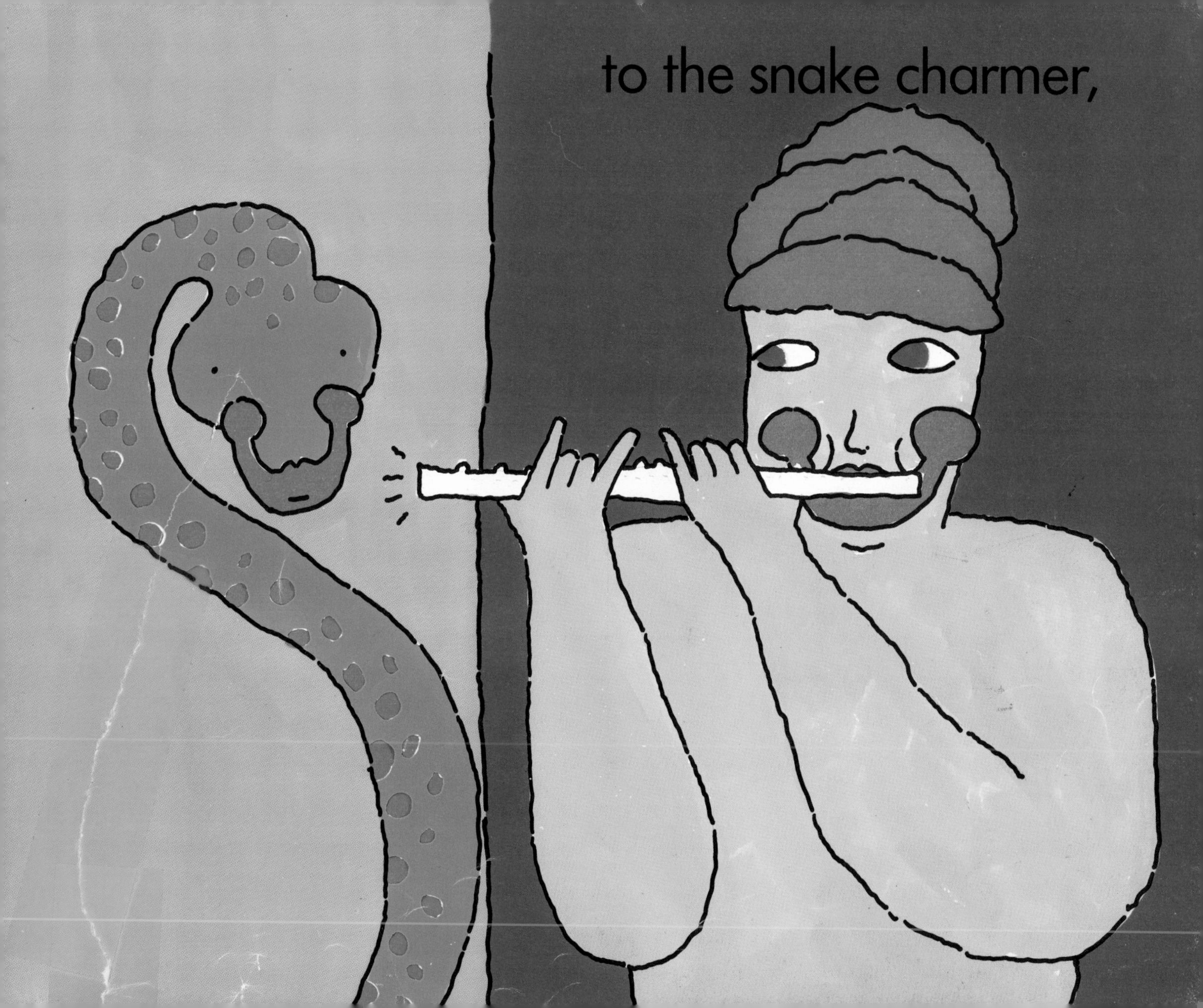

to the policeman
at the door,
then out the door
of the tent
and away.

The
clown
sat
down
and
cried.

Then all of a sudden,
in flew the smile
and landed on the clown,

and the circus went on.

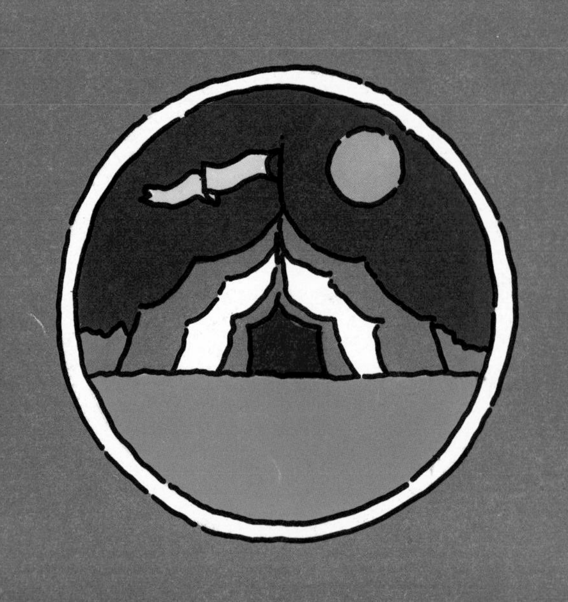